My Name Is James Madison Hemings

JONAH WINTER AND TERRY WIDENER

schwartz & wade books · new york

SLAVERY: when one human being owns another human being. To the owner, the enslaved person is often no more than a piece of property—a sheep, a horse, a "slave." But each enslaved person has a name, a mother, and a father—and a mind, a heart, and a story.

I know, because long ago I was born into slavery. This is my story.

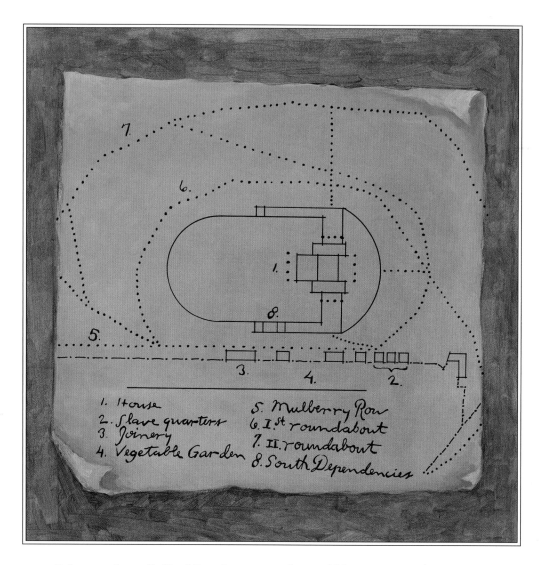

1. House
2. Slave quarters
3. Joinery
4. Vegetable Garden
5. Mulberry Row
6. I.st roundabout
7. II. roundabout
8. South Dependencies

My mother, Sally Hemings, was herself born into slavery, as had been her mother, my grandmother Elizabeth. On that Virginia plantation where we endured, my mother was housed in a shack with dirt floors—with my older brother and sister, Beverly and Harriet.

After I and my younger brother, Eston, were born, we were moved into the "dependencies," as they were called—two long rows of dungeon rooms beneath the terraces, built into the hillside, where horses were kept. We lived right next to the smokehouse, where meats were hung and smoked—Beverly, Harriet, Eston, Mother, and me, all in one tiny room.

Sometimes, though, we children were allowed to play inside the great house while our mother was at work there, cleaning up the chamber of her master, mending his clothes, making his bed.

I say "master," yet that is not all he was to me and my brothers and sister. I cannot recall precisely when I first became aware of our relation to this man who owned us. All I know is what my mother always said: "He is your father."

Many nights I lay awake, pondering this strange fact, looking out through the little window of our room at the distant stars.

Many days I sat outside on the grand lawn, staring at the beautiful mansion of this man. How could I be both his slave and his son?

One night, as Mother cooked us dinner, I asked her to explain: How could a father enslave his own flesh and blood? My mother had no answer. He was a most important man, she said. Someday I might know just how important. We dared not reveal we knew he was our father. This truth, self-evident, with our fair skin and father's looks, was never to be spoken of. Nor were we to mention the solemn pledge he had made to her some years ago, that he would free us as adults.

And so it went. When we were playing in his house, we were never to address him as Daddy. All we could do was stand there silently and watch while he tousled the hair of his white grandchildren. He had been married once, and his wife had died young. These were the children of his eldest daughter. They were our age. To them he gave the affection that he could not or would not give to us.

We did receive, however, somewhat special treatment.
Our father had promised our mother never to make us work
the fields that many others were forced to work. I remember
watching them and thinking: Unlike me, you will never be free.

And yet, my name was written in my father's "Farm Book"—the ledger where he recorded all his property. My brothers' and sister's names were also there, alongside the names of all the people he owned, right amongst the pages listing sheep and hogs. I can still picture him writing in that Farm Book. It wasn't until much later that I understood what he was writing.

As to the practical matter of managing his slaves, he left that up to his overseers—tough men who sometimes brandished whips.

And with his slaves out of view, my father would, upon occasion, play his violin.

Oh, how he adored his violin. He adored that violin so much that he gave us boys—my two brothers and me—violins of our own, which we taught ourselves how to play, with our older brother, Beverly, providing guidance.

And while our father assisted his grandchildren with their studies of English and Latin, giving them books, sharing his brilliance with them, my brothers and I were put to work. When each of us reached the age of twelve, we were sent to our uncle Johnny's workshop, assigned the task of helping him build chairs and tables and whatever other furniture our father wanted.

Uncle Johnny was a master carpenter, and he taught us everything he knew. This was *our* education.

I learned how to read and write from my father's granddaughter Ellen, who tutored me in those passing moments when I was not working.

During those moments, I could see my father off in the adjoining room, writing and writing and writing. I would not understand till many years later what he was writing—or how important his words were, or how important he was. After all, he was not one to boast.

My father was not one to show his emotions much at all—
at least, not to me. So even when my brothers and I built for him
beautiful pieces of furniture, I never knew if he was proud of us.

And the fact that we resembled him, especially as we grew older—was he secretly proud of this? Perhaps he did not know what he felt.

And what was I supposed to feel for my father, my "master"? What was I supposed to feel when he was very old, lying sick in bed, dying?

In the end, I was measurably grateful that my father kept his promise and freed Eston and me—just as he had freed my older siblings, Beverly and Harriet, four years earlier.

But our poor mother. Though she nursed our father through his final hours and was the mother of his children, he never freed her. Not long after Father died, Mother simply walked away with Eston and me, down the hill, never looking back. And no one ever tried to catch her.

But that was long ago, and she too is now dead and gone.

And I have long lived as a free man in the state of Ohio. My hair is now the color of snow.

Eston has passed away. And it has been many years since I last heard from Beverly or Harriet. They all changed their names and entered white communities, where no one ever guessed they were "tainted" with African blood. I suppose I could have done the same thing.

But a Hemings I was born, and a Hemings I remain—I bear my mother's name with pride. I am known far and wide for my carpentry skills. I built this barn and other buildings in town. Perhaps my father would be proud. I do not know.

But I do now understand just how important my father was. Not only was he president of the United States, he was also the man who wrote the Declaration of Independence. My father was none other than Thomas Jefferson.

All that I have of his are a few random trinkets my mother saved: a shoe buckle, a pair of eyeglasses, and an empty inkwell.

Who knows exactly what words he wrote with that ink. Perhaps they were those grand, inspiring words in the Declaration of Independence: *We hold these truths to be self-evident, that all men are created equal, that they are endowed by their Creator with certain unalienable rights, that among these are Life, Liberty, and the Pursuit of Happiness.* Or perhaps this ink was used to write slave names in his Farm Book. All I know is what I have told you here. This is my family history. And this is American history.

AUTHOR'S NOTE

James Madison Hemings, known as Madison, was born on January 19, 1805, on Thomas Jefferson's plantation, Monticello, in Virginia, and he died on November 28, 1877, in Huntington, Ross County, Ohio. He was the son of Sally Hemings, who was enslaved by Thomas Jefferson. Sally was the granddaughter of an enslaved African woman and an English sea captain named Hemings. They had a daughter, Elizabeth, who was owned by Jefferson's father-in-law, John Wayles. Sally was the daughter of Elizabeth and Wayles. As such, she was the half sister of Jefferson's deceased wife, Martha Wayles Jefferson. One quarter of her heritage was African—which meant that just one eighth of her children's heritage was African, making them very fair-skinned and legally "white" according to the laws of Virginia in the early 1800s. In an 1830 census, Madison was listed as "white." In an 1833 census, and all future ones, he was listed as "mulatto." That such arbitrary racist labels even exist is a topic for another book.

During Madison's childhood, there were rumors circulated by Jefferson's political enemies, some even printed in newspapers, that Jefferson was the father of all the Hemings children—rumors Jefferson never confirmed or denied. Some of Jefferson's admirers and white descendants have argued vigorously that such rumors were (and still are) ridiculous lies. But scientific evidence, based on DNA samples from Eston Hemings's descendants, has convinced most historians that Jefferson was indeed the father of Sally's children.

In many ways, Thomas Jefferson is one of the most impressive figures in American history. He owned and read more than sixty thousand books and spoke six languages. He was a president, an architect, an inventor, a farmer, a musician, and a writer. His writing promotes such noble ideals as education and religious freedom. And he did indeed write the Declaration of Independence. His words "All men are created equal" continue to inspire people and nations around the world.

But Jefferson's life and legacy are full of contradictions. He wrote beautifully about liberty and equality—and called slavery a "hideous blot." And as president, he outlawed the importation and enslavement of people from Africa. But he was also one of slavery's staunchest advocates and practitioners, and his halfhearted gestures toward gradual emancipation do not change this fact. He owned more than six hundred enslaved people throughout his life. He believed that people of African heritage were intellectually inferior to white people and that freed African Americans should be exiled to Africa.

While serving in the Virginia House of Burgesses before the Revolution, he tried to get a law passed that would have banished white mothers of mixed-race children—and all free African American children. And then there is the issue of his own enslaved children. These facts, alas, are all too often omitted from American history textbooks.

This book is inspired by and partially based on James Madison Hemings's 1873 newspaper interview in which he briefly summed up his family's story, including the bombshell that he was the son of Thomas Jefferson. He was the only one of Sally Hemings's children to go public with this claim.

Aside from this interview, there is limited documentation of Madison's childhood. To make it come alive for young readers, I've presented this story in a first-person narrative, as historical fiction, choosing to dramatize certain moments, such as the one in which Madison discovers that Jefferson was his father. Though Madison's interview makes no reference to it, my belief is that there would have been such a moment. Throughout the history of slavery, there were thousands of children whose fathers were also their owners. Every one of these children had to process this fact.

Other details from Madison's early life that I had to flesh out: who taught him how to read and write, how he came to own a violin, how he learned to play the violin, and whether he ever heard his father play the violin. Where proof is lacking, I have suggested what I believe to be most likely scenarios. Though Madison did not specify in his memoirs which white grandchildren helped him learn to read, it seems probable that Ellen did: she is known to have tutored other enslaved people, and Madison named one of his daughters after her. I have Jefferson giving Madison a violin, which seems possible; he loved the violin and gave musical instruments to his grandchildren. And I have Madison teaching himself how to play, which also seems possible.

I was able to piece together what Madison's life must have been like thanks to the groundbreaking work of historian Annette Gordon-Reed, whose writings on the Hemings family (and Jefferson's participation in that family) have changed our understanding of this topic.

Many celebratory books have been written about Thomas Jefferson. In writing this book about Madison Hemings, I wanted to present a different perspective on Jefferson's complex legacy—and to cast light on the life of a largely forgotten human being whose story has mainly been swept under the rug of history.

For Ta-Nehisi Coates —J.W.

For Liz, my discoverer and good friend. And to Anna Berkes, Lucia (Cinder)
Stanton, and Gaye Wilson, thank you for your help with this book. —T.W.

Text copyright © 2016 by Jonah Winter
Jacket art and interior illustrations copyright © 2016 by Terry Widener

All rights reserved. Published in the United States by Schwartz & Wade Books,
an imprint of Random House Children's Books, a division of Penguin Random House LLC, New York.

Schwartz & Wade Books and the colophon are trademarks of Penguin Random House LLC.

Visit us on the Web! randomhousekids.com

Educators and librarians, for a variety of teaching tools, visit us at RHTeachersLibrarians.com

Library of Congress Cataloging-in-Publication Data
Names: Winter, Jonah, author. | Widener, Terry, illustrator.
Title: My name is James Madison Hemings / by Jonah Winter ; illustrated by Terry Widener.
Description: First edition. | New York : Schwartz & Wade Books, 2016.
Identifiers: LCCN 2015036744 | ISBN 978-0-385-38342-4 (hardcover) | ISBN 978-0-385-38343-1 (glb) | ISBN 978-0-385-38344-8 (ebk)
Subjects: LCSH: Hemings, Madison, 1805–1877—Juvenile literature. | Jefferson, Thomas, 1743–1826—Relations with women—Juvenile literature.
Jefferson, Thomas, 1743–1826—Family—Juvenile literature. | Freedmen—Virginia—Biography—Juvenile literature.
Slaves—Virginia—Monticello—Biography—Juvenile literature. | Hemings, Sally—Juvenile literature.
Classification: LCC E332.2 .W58 2016 | DDC 973.4/6092 [B]—dc23

The text of this book is set in Bembo.
The illustrations were rendered in acrylic on bristol board.
Book design by Rachael Cole and Dasha Tolstikova.

MANUFACTURED IN CHINA
1 3 5 7 9 10 8 6 4 2
First Edition